A FAIR WIND FOR TROY
Doris Gates

Helen was the most beautiful woman the ancient world had
ever seen. When she chose Menelaus as her husband, the other
great chiefs vowed to band togther and make war against
anyone who dared steal her. But then Aphrodite, the goddess
of love, promised Paris of Troy the most beautiful woman
for his wife. Now the tragic prophecy that Paris would cause
the fall of Troy and the greatest war Greece had ever seen
began to be fulfilled.

Here also are the stories of:

Odysseus—the mortal who was as clever as Zeus
Agamemnon—forced to choose between his pledge to his
   brother and the life of his daughter
Clytemnestra—wife and murderer of Agamemnon
Achilles—greatest warrior in ancient Greece
Iphigenia—royal daughter and sacrifice to the gods

A
FAIR WIND
FOR TROY

DORIS GATES

Drawings by
CHARLES MIKOLAYCAK

Puffin Books

PUFFIN BOOKS
Published by the Penguin Group
Penguin Books USA Inc., 375 Hudson Street, New York, New York 10014, U.S.A.
Penguin Books Ltd, 27 Wrights Lane, London W8 5TZ, England
Penguin Books Australia Ltd, Ringwood, Victoria, Australia
Penguin Books Canada Ltd, 10 Alcorn Avenue, Toronto, Ontario, Canada M4V 3B2
Penguin Books (N.Z.) Ltd, 182–190 Wairau Road, Auckland 10, New Zealand

Penguin Books Ltd, Registered Offices: Harmondsworth, Middlesex, England

First published by The Viking Press 1976
Published in Puffin Books 1984
10   9
Text copyright © 1976 by Viking Penguin Inc.
Illustrations copyright © 1976 by Viking Penguin Inc.

Library of Congress Cataloging in Publication Data
Gates, Doris, 1901–   A fair wind for Troy.
"Puffin books."
Summary: Retells the events leading up to the Trojan
War including Helen's capture by Paris and the
sacrifice of Iphigenia at Aulis.
1. Trojan War—Juvenile literature.   2. Mythology,
Greek—Juvenile literature.   [1. Trojan War.   2. Mythology,
Greek]   I. Mikolaycak, Charles, ill.   II. Title.
BL793.T7G37   1984   292'.13   [398.2]   83-43167   ISBN 0 14 03.1718 X

Printed in the United States of America

CONTENTS

THE OATH

*T*he great palace at Sparta was buzzing with activity. Always a busy place, now it seemed to swarm with slaves, all hurrying about their appointed tasks. King Tyndareus was expecting guests.

His youngest daughter, Helen, had arrived at a marriageable age, thus presenting a problem to the king, a really difficult one. By all accounts she was considered to be the most beautiful woman in the world; her suitors numbered in the scores, and among them were the most powerful young chiefs in all Greece. To make enemies of most of them by giving Helen's hand to one of them could bring about an attack on Sparta that could well cost Tyndareus his kingdom.

It was Odysseus who came to the old king's rescue. Odysseus the wily; Odysseus the clever; Odysseus, a counselor equal to Zeus; Odysseus whose wanderings recorded by Homer in *The Odyssey* would make him the most famous of all the Greeks who fought before the walls of Troy.

Already aware of the young man's insightfulness, Tyndareus had summoned him from Ithaca to ask his advice.

"Something must be done about Helen," Tyndareus informed the young chief. "The fame of her beauty has spread throughout the whole of Greece. As you know, she has already been kidnapped once by Theseus, and her brothers brought her back unharmed. It could happen again. She must have a husband to protect her. But I fear that the moment I bestow her hand upon one, all you others will wage war against me and together you will destroy me."

Odysseus smiled wryly. He, too, wanted Helen's hand, but not with much hope. His kingdom was poor compared to the others—a small rocky island, inhospitable to horses. "I assume from what you have just said that you have not considered me as her future protector."

Tyndareus cleared his throat in some embarrassment. "I admire you very much, Odysseus, and I have brought you here to seek your advice. But let us be practical. Your kingdom is small, your ships few. Suppose some powerful chief decided to take her from you by force. How would you prevent it?"

Odysseus shrugged and again smiled wryly. "You are doubtless right, Tyndareus," he said. "And the beautiful and much-courted Helen would find life on tiny Ithaca hardly to her liking."

"Yes, she is spoiled," said Tyndareus, "but what beautiful woman is not? And they are always a problem. Sometimes I wish she were as hideous as a Harpy."

Odysseus laughed. "The world would be the poorer for that," he declared. "Such loveliness as Helen's is well worth whatever its cost may be. Had fate so ordained, I would gladly have accepted its risks."

"That's all very well," grumbled Tyndareus, "but how am I to handle the problem of her marriage?"

"Quite simply. Summon all the suitors here and make them swear that they will not attempt to take Helen away from her chosen husband. Then let Helen make her own choice of a husband. That way they will have no excuse for an attack upon you."

For the first time in many a month, Tyndareus smiled. The frown he had worn between his bristling brows suddenly erased itself, and all the lines of his face mellowed. "You've hit upon the very thing, Odysseus. I knew you would. What a pity your kingdom isn't wider and your powers greater! I could have used a son-in-law like you." Then his face clouded again. "But suppose they won't take the oath?"

"Then Helen will live and die husbandless."

The old king laughed. "A likely possibility! But it will prove a useful threat. Each will be hopeful that she will choose him and in that hope will take the oath."

"Furthermore," continued Odysseus, "you must make them swear that if any one abducts Helen from her chosen husband, the rest will band together and make war against him in an effort to bring Helen back."

"Indeed, yes," agreed Tyndareus. "And it shall be a most solemn oath."

"Of course," said Odysseus.

So the young chiefs were summoned from all over Greece to meet at the palace at Sparta. Among these came Menelaus, accompanied by his brother, Agamemnon, king of Mycenae. These two were the wealthiest and most powerful chiefs in all Greece.

Helen's beauty was so astonishing as to seem scarcely mortal. Nor was it altogether mortal. She was a daughter of Zeus, who had fallen in love with her mother, Leda, and had wooed her in the form of a swan. When the time for Leda's delivery was at hand, she gave birth to two large eggs, swan's eggs. They broke open and twin boys were discovered in one. A most beautiful baby girl rolled out of the other: Helen of Troy had come into the world. The twins were named Castor and Polydeuces, and were referred to thereafter as the Dioscuri.

An older daughter, Clytemnestra, was the child of Tyndareus and Leda and wife of Agamemnon.

The suitors spent two days feasting and gaming with Tyndareus before Helen was sent for. Some of the lesser chiefs had become hopelessly drunk on the old king's wine, possibly to drown their despair when they beheld the rich robes, the gilded chariots, and the high-stepping horses of the two brothers from Mycenae. Who could compete with them? It was clear from the beginning that Agamemnon was there to put in a good word for his brother with his father-in-law. Tyndareus was scrupulously courteous to each in turn and, of course, none knew that Helen, herself, was to choose her future husband. During these two days she had been closeted with her sister, Clytemnestra, who, brought here by her husband for the purpose, made the most of this opportunity to describe to her younger sister the wonders of life in the great palace of Mycenae.

"Surely our father will see the wisdom of bestowing your hand upon my brother-in-law, Menelaus," said Clytemnestra, her dark eyes searching Helen's as if she might read the future there.

"But would he dare to marry both his daughters into a single kingdom? Besides, Menelaus has no kingdom; the throne at Mycenae is Agamemnon's," Helen reminded her.

What Clytemnestra did not know was that Helen had never been really fond of this elder sister. Her dark beauty was attractive and in no way a threat to Helen's dazzling loveliness. But there was also a dark intensity about her, an almost brooding fierceness, that Helen found repellent. There was no humor in her, no flippant charm, no playfulness whatsoever. Life at Mycenae with Clytemnestra for companionship could be a suffocating experience, Helen thought, despite the wealth that Menelaus could bestow upon her in the way of gowns and jewels and slaves. Yet Menelaus as brother of Agamemnon was undoubtedly one of the most powerful men in Greece. Her position as his wife would be only a little less favorable than Clytemnestra's. And he was undoubtedly handsome. With her sister, Helen had stolen once from the women's quarters during the first day of the gathering and, peering from behind a pillar, her veil carefully shielding her face, had studied him with interest when Clytemnestra had pointed him out to her. Tall, broad-shouldered, his head set proudly and his eyes flashing confidence, he looked every inch the warrior. She thought she could manage to live quite happily with such a husband. If only he had a kingdom of his own and she could be, like her sister, an undisputed queen!

At last the day came when Helen was summoned to the throne room where Tyndareus and his guests were gathered. She dressed herself carefully for this occasion, wearing a white gown of linen so fine that its draperies were like spider web. A white silk veil shot through with threads of gold clung to her head and cascaded down around her shoulders. Surrounded by her maidens and moving silently on golden sandals, she entered the great hall.

The old king saw her first, and as the crowd of suitors turned to see what had caught his attention, sudden silence enveloped the room. She paused, awaiting her father's summons, and few men there but felt an anguish of longing to possess this radiant creature. Her bearing was queenly, neither shy nor bold. Added to this was a quiet assurance and dignity that can come only to those who know their worth, are aware of any admiration accorded it, and accept the homage without a trace of false modesty. Helen well knew that her beauty held a special quality, a goddess-like perfection, and now as she faced her father and her suitors she felt its power and smiled into their eyes. Tyndareus raised a hand and beckoned her toward him where he sat upon his throne. Leaving her maidens clustered at the hall's entrance, Helen advanced into the hall, moving with stately grace, her garments swirling and clinging about her.

Tyndareus rose as she approached the throne, and he himself seated her with formal courtesy in a low chair nearby.

"Helen," he said, "I think you know why you have been summoned here today."

She inclined her head and her veil fell forward, modestly concealing her face.

"The time has come for you to choose a husband from among these young men gathered here."

She looked up quickly at him and the veil fell back, revealing her perfect profile to the room. "I am to choose?" she asked.

"You are to choose," he said firmly and a murmur went around the hall. This was most unusual! New hope leaped in hearts that had been despairing only moments before. Agamemnon turned to his brother with an eager smile, which Menelaus chose not to notice.

"But before you make your choice, my daughter, I have some words to say to all gathered here. Before Helen bestows her hand, each man of you must swear to accept her choice and make no vengeful war upon her husband." The silence in the hall was intense as the old king continued. "And you must further swear that if any man should abduct Helen from her husband, you will come with your ships and your warriors to aid him in recovering her."

The silence was broken by a sudden shout of affirmation, but Tyndareus was not to be satisfied with such a general acceptance. Each man was to swear individually, his oath witnessed by all. The old king rose and led the company into the courtyard beyond the great hall, where a priest of Poseidon held—with difficulty—a frightened and rearing stallion. He was a noble beast, and now he was to be sacrificed to the god as part of the oath-taking ceremony.

When all the men were gathered in the courtyard—Helen and her maidens had remained in the hall—the priest seized a long knife and with one swift, practiced stroke cut the stallion's throat. There was an awesome gush of blood, and the beautiful creature slumped to the pavement, his legs crumpled under him. He was hardly dead when the priest's assistants began swarming over the carcass, dismembering it. Then the suitors each in turn stood upon a piece of the dead horse and swore the required oath—not to make war upon Helen's husband and to come to his aid if anyone should abduct her from him.

After the oath-taking they all returned to the throne room, where again Tyndareus spoke. "A final word," he said, "and then Helen shall make her choice. I shall bestow my kingdom and my crown upon the man she chooses. The husband of Helen shall become ruler of Sparta. Let gods and men be witness to this promise. And now, my daughter"—he smiled fondly at the beautiful girl looking up at him with astonished eyes—"now you shall make your choice."

She rose and placed a hand on the back of her chair. For the first time since she had entered the hall she showed uncertainty.

"Why should you renounce your throne?" she asked.

"My dear, I am old and I would gladly pass the responsibilities of this kingdom to someone else. I had, of course, expected that your brothers would succeed me, but Castor and Polydeuces are dead, and so I have decided my son-in-law shall have my throne."

The twin brothers, after joining the Argonauts in their search for the Golden Fleece, had journeyed to the country of two cattle owners, Idas and Lynceus. There Castor quarreled with Idas, who stabbed him to death. Polydeuces was overcome with grief at the death of his brother and begged to be allowed to die with him. Zeus kindly allowed the brothers to share in the life and death of each. Half their time would be spent in Hades and half on high Olympus. In our night sky two stars are associated with them: the constellation Gemini, the Twins.

But Helen was not thinking of her brothers' fate as she considered with mounting interest the old king's decision. His words had put an entirely different light on the matter of her marriage. Come what might, she would be a queen, and as this certainty sank in, her eyes sought those of Menelaus.

He was standing not far from her, Agamemnon having maneuvered him as close to the throne as propriety allowed.

As their eyes met and held, a blush mounted in Helen's face, and she hid behind her veil. But only for a moment.

Then, lifting her head and tossing the veil aside, she flung out an arm, imperiously pointing to Menelaus.

"I choose him," she declared in a voice light and girlish, but ringing with perfect certainty.

Like one stunned, Menelaus stood helplessly staring at her, unable to believe his luck until Agamemnon, with a triumphant laugh, slapped him on the shoulder. "Why do you hesitate?" he demanded. "Must the lady come to you?"

Dazedly Menelaus moved forward. At the same time, Tyndareus rose from his throne and gently took Helen's hand. Menelaus put out his own, and the old king laid hers in it. Looking steadfastly into the eyes of his future wife, Menelaus raised her hand to his lips.

Now there was confusion in the hall. Many of the disappointed suitors, unable to endure the sight of the Mycenaeans' triumph, left abruptly, summoning horses and chariots for the return home. But others less willing to risk an insult to the hospitality of Tyndareus, to say nothing of Menelaus, stayed to celebrate the wedding feast.

For many years Helen and Menelaus lived happily together in Sparta. A daughter, Hermione, was born to them. In time Hermione would become the bride of great Achilles' son. But the years grew monotonous for the beauteous Helen. Marriage and motherhood became humdrum. While her beauty was as famed as ever, with her husband's jealous eyes upon her there were few to pay her compliments. Besides, she had spent all her life in Sparta. Even a queen can become bored with the sameness of daily duties, the same faces in the same halls, the same all-too-familiar landscape beyond those halls.

Then one evening as Helen and her husband sat in their

private room, he recounting the adventures of that day's hunt and she busy with some needlework, a servant entered and announced the arrival of a stranger at the palace gates.

"He says his name is Paris and that he is a son of Priam, king of Troy," said the servant.

Menelaus rose, pleased. "We are honored to receive a son of Priam," he told the servant, while Helen looked up with sudden interest. "Bring him in; bring him in at once."

THE ABDUCTION
OF HELEN

*T*he city of Troy was situated on a hill overlooking a large plain through which flowed the Scamander River on its way to the sea. Many cities had once risen where now stood the walls surrounding Troy, over which King Priam ruled. The city was old and it was rich, commanding as it did the entrance to the Hellespont, the strait connecting what is now the Aegean Sea with the Sea of Marmara. Ships arriving from the southern ocean and wanting to pass through the straits to the east were often detained near the mouth of the Scamander by adverse winds. While waiting for a favorable wind, they exhausted their water supplies. In order to refill their water casks, they were forced to pay tribute to Priam. This tribute made up a considerable part of Troy's revenue. Besides this, every ship entering the Hellespont from east or west was forced to pay toll to Troy. Hence the city was resented and envied by a large number of other city-kingdoms. Yet none dared make war against Troy, for her walls, built by Apollo and Poseidon, were impregnable. Only the mighty Heracles in the time of Priam's father had succeeded in disciplining Troy. Ultimately the city was destined to fall, but through trickery, not by force of arms.

A few years before Helen was hatched from a swan's egg, a baby boy had been born to Queen Hecuba of Troy. He was a healthy, promising babe, but there was no celebration over his birth. Before her delivery Hecuba had had a dream in which she gave birth to a firebrand. Priam, calling in a seer to interpret the dream, received the dread prophecy that the expected child would be a son who would cause the ruin of the city. Through him its towers would be burned and its palace sacked.

Immediately following the birth, the royal parents held council together and came to a dreadful decision. The new little prince must be put to death.

"He is such a splendid baby," mourned Hecuba, knowing that her words would in no way weaken her husband's determination. Nor did she really want the baby to be spared. This was a child of ill omen and as such must be gotten rid of before it could do mischief.

"We have another son," was Priam's cold comfort. He was referring to the baby's older brother, Hector.

So the baby was given into the hands of one of Priam's shepherds named Agelaus with orders to kill him. But Agelaus, gazing upon the perfect small body lying in his arms, felt his heart touched, and he could not bring himself to destroy the child. Instead, he took him to Mount Ida and there abandoned him on a bank of moss. But instead of starving or being killed by wild animals, the baby was kept alive by a she-bear who came each day to suckle it. When after five days Agelaus returned to the spot where he had left the child, expecting to find it dead, he saw it happily waving its small hands in the air and cooing contentedly. He also saw the she-bear, which shuffled off at his approach. Agelaus realized at once how things stood and decided that the gods had taken a hand in this babe's destiny. He took the child to his own humble dwelling, named him Paris, and reared him as a son.

By the time Paris had grown to young manhood, he had added another name to the one the shepherd had given him. His comrades called him Alexander, or conqueror, for his brave resistance against the robbers and wild beasts that came to attack their flocks and herds.

It was while he was herding sheep and cattle on the gentle slopes of Mount Ida that Paris won the love of Oenone, daughter of a river god. He lived happily with her for several years, and then his destiny was changed by a wedding in Thessaly, a province in northern Greece.

Thetis was the daughter of Nereus, a sea god, and Doris, an ocean nymph. She was considered the loveliest of all her sister Nereids, and both Poseidon and Zeus fell in love with her. Before the two brothers could settle their dispute over which should claim the beautiful sea-creature, they were warned by Prometheus, a Titan with the gift of prophecy, that she would bear a son who would turn out to be greater than his father. Neither Zeus nor Poseidon wanted to risk such an outcome of their wooing, and so they both agreed that the lovely Thetis should for the sake of all Olympus be married to a mortal.

They chose for her spouse the son of the king of Thessaly, Peleus by name. He was considered to be in every way one of the most deserving young men in all Greece. Thetis was not happy to be the bride of a mere mortal, but Zeus had commanded, and not even her father, Nereus, could withstand the will of the Father of Gods. So the marriage was held and the wedding feast celebrated.

It was a brilliant affair. All the gods and goddesses attended. The only Immortal not invited was a dreary hag named Eris, goddess of discord. True to her name, she had thought of a way to avenge this slight to her dignity.

All the happy company was assembled around the long table. Zeus and Hera sat at its head, and the bride and groom sat together at the other end—Peleus handsome and triumphant, Thetis subdued, even brooding. She, too, had the gift of prophecy and already knew that this marriage promised no good to anyone.

Suddenly in the midst of all the toasts and merrymaking, a golden apple was flung into the center of the long table, where it rolled, glittering, before it came to a stop. For a moment there was the silence of complete surprise, and then Hermes reached a hand and retrieved the golden fruit.

"There is writing on it," he declared, looking toward Zeus.

"What does it say?" demanded the Father of Gods.

"It says, 'To the Fairest,'" Hermes replied.

"Then give it to me," said Hera, rising from her seat beside her husband and reaching an arm toward Hermes, who still held the shining apple in his hand.

Pallas Athena sprang from her seat. "One moment," she cried. "As goddess of wisdom I am, of course, the fairest. The apple belongs to me, for what is fairer than wisdom?"

"Not so," declared Aphrodite, also rising. "I am the goddess of love and beauty. There can be no question that this golden treasure should be mine."

Watching from behind a column, Eris, goddess of discord,

listened to the dispute, a cruel smile on her lips. Then, unseen and unsuspected, she glided from the hall.

Now all three goddesses had turned toward Zeus, each talking at once, their eyes flashing angrily, their voices shrill, and demanded that he choose among them.

But what god or man would willingly accept the risk of such a judgment? Zeus eyed the angry goddesses and knew that there would be no peace for him on high Olympus if he chose among them. So now he raised his hand and demanded silence. He seized Hera's wrist and drew her down into her chair again. The other two then seated themselves, but the faces of all three were unrelenting as they faced the Lord of the Sky.

"This is not a judgment I care to make," he explained. "However, that there must be a judgment is beyond dispute. Therefore, I shall send Hermes, my swift-footed son, to the slopes of Mount Ida, where a certain shepherd tends his flocks. He is the handsomest of all men on earth. His name is Paris, and he shall, himself, decide which one of you three great goddesses is the fairest. His decision will be final."

So the matter was left for the moment, and the feasting continued. Only now the bride was not the only one at that board who wore a brooding look.

The eventual birth of a son did little to relieve Thetis's unhappiness, for the Fates decreed a harsh destiny for him. He could either live a long and humdrum life without fame or special honor, or he could live a short and glorious one. Thetis knew that this child, whom she named Achilles, would choose the latter. And so, to thwart the Fates, she decided to make him immortal like herself.

For this purpose it was necessary to immerse him in flame even as Demeter did the infant Domophoön. She anointed her baby's body with ambrosia and each night for several nights laid him on a fire. But one night Peleus surprised her as she performed the rite.

Appalled at the sight, Peleus rushed forward and seized his son, burning his own hands cruelly in the flames. But Achilles seemed none the worse for his exposure to them.

"What idiot sacrifice is this?" demanded the outraged father.

"Fool!" replied Thetis. "Fool mortal! Little you know of your son's destiny. Had you not interfered, all his mortality would have been burned out of him and he would have become immortal, as is his mother."

With these words, the furious nymph fled from her husband's house and returned to Nereus, her father, in the watery depths of ocean.

There is another version of Thetis's attempt to immortalize her son which has special meaning for us today. According to this later legend, she dipped him in the waters of the River Styx, the stream on which the souls of the dead are borne to Hades. But since she held the infant by one ankle, which did not become immersed in the water, this part of Achilles' body continued to be mortal and vulnerable to hurt. Eventually, the great hero (for Achilles grew up to become the greatest hero in all Greece) was killed during the Trojan War by an arrow shot into this mortal heel. It was Paris who shot the arrow, but Apollo guided its flight. Since that time we use the term "Achilles' heel" to indicate liability to danger or vulnerability. Moreover, the strong tendon joining the muscles of the calf of the leg to the bone of the heel is called Achilles' tendon.

Left now with an infant son on his hands, Peleus considered what he should do with him. He wanted the best for the child, like any father, but felt inadequate to provide it. Then he remembered the good centaur, Cheiron, who had reared the great hunter, Actaeon, and Jason, leader of the Argonauts, with whom he, Peleus, had gone in search of the Golden Fleece. Besides, when treachery had once threatened to destroy his life on the slopes of Mount Pelion, where Cheiron made his home, the wise centaur had saved Peleus's life. Perhaps Cheiron would be willing to place Peleus further in his debt by rearing his small son, Achilles.

Cheiron proved more than willing. He welcomed the child, and as soon as Achilles was old enough, Cheiron began to instruct him in the arts of weaponry and hunting. He also taught him to play the lyre.

On a certain slope of Mount Ida the sun laid slanting shadows aslant the grass. Here in the pleasant shade a shepherd lay, his back resting against a mossy bank. It was well past midday, and his flock, their bellies full of the sweet fodder, reclined about him, forefeet tucked neatly under them, and woolly sides dappled with sun and shade. The shepherd was young and handsome enough to be a king's son, though he wore a simple tunic belted at the waist. Crude sandals protected the soles of his feet. He was indeed a king's son, though he did not know it, and his name was Paris.

Suddenly all shadows within the grove were banished in a blinding light, and there appeared before Paris the god Hermes, wearing his winged sandals, his broad hat, and with his herald's staff in his hand.

Paris sprang to his feet, startled by the blinding light, his heart leaping with the certain knowledge that a god stood before him.

"Hail, Paris, and fear not," Hermes greeted him. "I am

sent by Zeus." He reached out a hand in which lay a golden apple. "Zeus commands that you make judgment as to which one is the fairest of three goddesses. They are Hera, Athena, and Aphrodite. You are to bestow this golden apple on the goddess you choose."

Paris was filled with foreboding as he heard the god's words. How could he, a mere mortal, decide among three such powerful goddesses? And no matter whom he chose, it would be his fate to incur the wrath of the other two. It was not fair that Zeus should place such a burden upon him. He began to voice his doubts.

"How can the Father of Gods expect me to judge these goddesses when I have never laid eyes on them?" he protested.

"That objection can be quickly remedied," said Hermes, and putting out his hand, he led into the presence of the amazed shepherd the three most powerful goddesses on Olympus: Hera, Athena, and Aphrodite.

Paris paled at the sight. "Truly," he protested further, "I have no wish to choose among you. Let someone worthier than I have this honor."

"Zeus has spoken," Hermes reminded him, "and there is no way you can shirk the duty he has laid upon you. Here and now you will decide who is to possess the golden apple which bears the words, 'To the Fairest.' "

"Then let them stand before me one at a time," said Paris, "for I am bedazzled by the sight of all three at once and could in no wise make up my mind."

"It shall be done as you wish," said Hermes.

With the words, he led off to one side of the glen Athena and Aphrodite, leaving Hera facing Paris alone.

"I am Hera," she declared, "wife of Zeus and as such high queen of all Heaven. If you will name me the fairest, Paris, I

promise that you shall become the greatest king the world has ever known. You will be all-powerful, and men will recognize the power of your name for ages to come. Riches will accompany the power. You will be great indeed if you choose me."

Paris's eyes lighted at her words. Though his shepherd's life was a happy one, the lure of power was great. Yes, he would choose Hera. But still he must inspect the other two in all fairness. So Hera withdrew and Hermes led forward Athena.

"Paris," began the goddess when she and the shepherd were alone, "I am Athena, goddess of war and wisdom. If you will choose me, I promise that you will become the greatest warrior the world has ever known. And wise beyond all mortals. Men's tongues will recount your valor down the ages, and the fame of your name will never die."

Paris considered her words. A king's power was great, yet a warrior's honor greater still. He thought of Heracles and Theseus, of Jason and Perseus. How marvelous to have a name as famed as one of these! Yes, he would choose Athena and live forever in the minds of men.

But there was one goddess yet to account for. Hermes led Aphrodite before Paris and departed with Athena at his side.

For a long moment Aphrodite looked upon Paris. No words came from her lips, now wreathed in a smile so beguiling that Paris felt a strange stirring within him. She sidled close to him, so close that the shepherd blushed at the nearness of her rosy flesh. She laughed a silvery peal that carried across the glade to where the others waited.

"Paris, I know not what the other two have promised you, for certain it is that they have sought to bribe you. But what I have to offer no man can resist. If you will award me the golden apple I promise you the most beautiful woman in the world for your wife. She is Helen, wife of Menelaus of Sparta, and her beauty is second only to my own."

"But how can she become my wife if she is already another man's?"

"That is of small significance," the goddess replied airily. "Already she is bored with her lot. Once her eyes have fallen on you, she will feel such a surge of passion that she will willingly go off with you. You have only to await an opportunity when her husband is not around to take her away. Then such a life of enchantment shall be yours as will make you the envy of every man alive."

"Do you promise that this will come to pass?" he asked.

"I swear it on the Styx," said Aphrodite, and her face was suddenly solemn. The River Styx carried the souls of dead mortals to Hades, and not even a god could swear on it and go against his oath.

Without further word, Paris placed the golden apple in her hand.

Aphrodite forthwith ascended to high Olympus, a smile of triumph on her sweet lips. But Hera and Athena, their arms linked, strode off angrily, muttering terrible threats against Paris and all connected with him.

Not long after this judgment, Priam sent some herders to Mount Ida to select a bull from among the cattle pastured there. It must be a fine animal, for it was to be given as a prize in the funeral games which he held each year honoring a dead son.

Now the bull chosen was from Paris's own herd, and it was a favorite of his. He had tamed it and groomed it until its sides shone like satin. When the herders started to lead the bull away, Paris went after them, pleading with them to take some other animal.

"But Priam has ordered us to bring him the best, and this bull is undoubtedly the best to be seen anywhere around here. Whoever wins this bull in the games will be well rewarded for his efforts," they told him.

Games! The word caught Paris's attention. Why should he not go and compete himself? He was young, strong, and although he was not skilled, his valor might make up for what he lacked in knowledge. And if he won, the bull would again be his.

So Paris accompanied the herders to Troy and there took part in the games. Priam's other sons and the best young men in the city competed against him. But in every event the strength and courage of the young shepherd won over them. At last, enraged that this nobody, this ignorant shepherd, should be the victor of this year's games, they set upon him with their weapons and would have killed Paris had he not raced for an altar of Zeus at the edge of the field and, gaining it before his enemies could overtake him, invoked the god's name to protect himself.

It was at this point that the old shepherd who had first discovered Paris as an abandoned infant and taken him home to rear him as a son now ran toward where King Priam sat watching the contests.

"Priam," he cried, "King, listen to me, I beg." Guards sprang forward to seize the old man, but he threw himself on the ground at Priam's feet and the king raised a hand, indicating that he should be let alone. "This young man who has defeated all in the contests today is your rightful son. It is no shame that he has bested all the princes of Troy here today, for he is, himself, a prince."

Then the old shepherd, greatly fearing, related how he had abandoned this son of Priam, instead of killing him, and how he had found him alive and had taken him home to rear as his own son. His voice trembled as he made the confession, for such disobedience could cost him his life.

But Priam, pleased at this youth's prowess and happy to have such a fine son restored to him, raised old Agelaus from the dust and summoned Paris to his embrace. Forgotten was the fearful prophecy, for who could see calamity in a young man so handsome and of such promise? Paris was welcomed back into the palace and restored to his rightful dignity as a prince of Troy.

Before long Paris's brothers began urging him to marry. They knew nothing of the fact that he was already married to the nymph Oenone. Even if they had known, they would have wanted for their young brother a wife more substantial than the daughter of a river god.

At length Paris told them of Aphrodite's promise and urged his father to give him a ship to sail to Sparta and take away Helen to be his wife. Priam was not so averse to this as one might have expected him to be. Some years before, Telemon had made off with Priam's sister, Hesione, and taken her to Greece. Despite Priam's threats and pleas, he had refused to return the princess. Now it seemed to Priam only just retribution that a son of his should seize a Greek's wife. But Cassandra, Priam's prophetic daughter, foretold dire consequences for Troy if Paris set out on such an expedition. And when he told Oenone of his plan, she, too, warned him of a dreadful fate if he should succeed in stealing the wife of Menelaus.

"I would expect you to say that," Paris told her.

They stood together in a leafy glade close to the spot where Agelaus, the shepherd, had discovered the abandoned babe.

"Nothing you can say, Oenone, will make any difference to me. My heart is set on having Helen for my wife."

"Why do you wish to abandon me?" asked the nymph, her eyes filling with tears. "Have I not loved you well and faithfully? Am I, too, not fair?"

Noting her tears, for a moment Paris's selfish heart was moved. He took her in his arms and held her close.

"You have been a good and faithful wife, and surely you are fair and I have loved you, Oenone. But now try to understand. No longer am I a shepherd—I am a powerful king's son. I must have a wife to help me fill this role. Aphrodite has promised me Helen, the most beautiful woman on earth. Already she is a queen, knowledgeable in the ways of royalty. She will have dignity as well as beauty; she will be a fitting consort for a prince. You have been my playfellow, my dear delight here in these woodland places. But how could you endure life in a palace? How could you expect to be accepted by my queenly mother and her royal daughters? Each day would be a long humiliation for you. I would spare you this suffering."

Oenone clung to him. "Such suffering would be nothing compared to what I shall endure when you have left me," she sobbed. Then, summoning a trace of dignity, she drew away from him, dashed the tears from her eyes, and swallowed her sobs. "Very well, Paris." She spoke quietly now. "There remains one more thing to be said. I have the power of healing as well as of prophecy. If you are ever wounded, come to me, for only I can heal you."

"I promise you I will," said Paris, and, turning away, went quickly off through the aisles of trees as if eager to outdistance any last spoken word of hers. And he never looked back.

But when, years later, Paris was wounded during the Trojan War by one of the poisoned arrows of Heracles and sought Oenone's help, she refused it and he died. Bitterness had grown in her heart, and her hatred of Helen had consumed all her former love for Paris. Yet, when she learned of his death, remorse so overwhelmed her reason that she hanged herself.

Paris did not meet Helen on that first evening of his arrival in Sparta. In accordance with the custom of that time, his host would appraise the stranger before he would be introduced to the ladies of the court. But when at last they did meet, Aphrodite was as good as her word. In the first moment that their eyes met, it was settled between them, and Paris knew beyond a doubt that this woman who stood before him, fairer to his eyes even than Aphrodite, would be his when the proper moment came to claim her.

The moment was not long in coming. Some nine days after Paris had arrived, word reached Menelaus that his grandfather had died on the island of Crete and would be buried there. He must, of course, attend the ceremonies. Since Crete lay in the southern Aegean, about two hundred miles south and east of the mainland, and Sparta was fifty miles inland from the sea, it would be a long time before Menelaus could be back in his palace again.

"I depend on you to entertain our guest," he told Helen. "Make sure that he has all the hunting and feasting his young heart desires. It is unfortunate that I must absent myself at this time, but duty presses. Paris has been most graciously understanding of my need to leave him. I hope your hospitality toward him will leave nothing to be desired."

Helen's reply was all that a husband could wish. "I am sure he will find my company a poor substitute for yours, Menelaus, but I shall do what I can to keep warm the welcome you have given him."

Menelaus took a casually affectionate and hasty farewell of his wife and hastened to his waiting chariot. It would be ten years before he saw her again.

Paris and Helen moved quickly after his departure. They estimated the time it would take Menelaus to reach the coast and outfit his ship. When they were sure he was sailing toward Crete, they made ready their own escape.

Paris had entertained some doubts about Helen's daughter, Hermione. The little girl was now nine years old. A child had not figured in his plans, but would Helen abandon her willingly?

Helen soon put his doubts to rest. "The child means nothing to me," she declared. Indeed, during the long months of pregnancy when her body had become swollen and distorted with the life growing inside her, Helen had known an agony of fear. Would she ever be beautiful again? Would this thickened waist ever return to its former elegant proportions? At the time of her betrothal, Menelaus had encircled it with his two hands. Now the grossest of her slave girls was more lissome than she.

But Helen, favorite of Aphrodite, had risen from her childbed as irresistible as ever. There had been no visible evidence that she needed the oils and unguents with which her belly was daily massaged. Still, Helen had taken no chances, and she had known well how Sparta's athletes cared for their bodies.

So her desertion of this daughter who had caused her such anxiety brought no pangs at all to this mother's heart.

The day before their departure, Paris put a question to his love. "When your sister Clytemnestra left this palace as the bride of Agamemnon, did she not take rich treasure with her as her dowry?"

Helen looked sharply at him. "I was too young to be aware

of my father's arrangements at that time," she informed him. She added with obvious satisfaction, "Clytemnestra, you know, is considerably older than I."

Paris stood lost in thought for a moment, tugging at his lower lip. "Your father turned over his kingdom to Menelaus —this palace with its rich furnishings, his slaves, his horses and herds. But had you gone to Mycenae as his bride, a dowry would have gone with you. Would it not seem right, then, that you should take away with you what would in other cir- cumstances have been yours? Menelaus will, after all, have your father's kingdom. You should have something of what is yours by birth and right."

Helen heartily agreed. She even admired her lover's shrewd- ness. "This had not occurred to me," she admitted. "How fortunate for us both that you can keep a level head, Paris, despite the present turmoil in your heart."

In answer, Paris drew her into his arms while his eyes ap- praised the richness of the room's furnishings.

When at last they departed for the coast, two well-laden wagons of plunder from the palace went with them. The slow trip across the Spartan plain and over the mountains to where Paris's ship awaited them seemed interminable to Helen. The jolting vehicle in which she rode, padded though it was, wearied her. It was sweet to have Paris riding beside her, en- couraging her with honeyed words of love. But she feared that by some foul chance Menelaus might learn of their escape and send his minions after them. She was impatient to see Troy, a bustling city on a busy trade route, its court certain to be more alive and vital than that of isolated Sparta. Would they accept her there? And if they did, would Priam risk war with the Argives in order to keep her?

She was safe on both counts. Priam welcomed her warmly

and, marveling at her beauty, declared that never should she be allowed to return to her former husband. The old king and all the people of Troy seemed to have fallen in love with her beauty. Not even the threat of war—for surely Menelaus would try to recapture her—could dim their pride in having this lovely creature for their very own. Helen accepted the adulation as her just due.

THE GATHERING
OF THE CHIEFS

News of his wife's flight with Paris from Sparta reached Menelaus while he was still in Crete. The announcement came from Hera. She hated Aphrodite, who had received the golden apple as the fairest among the three goddesses, and she hated Paris for that judgment. So she sent Iris, goddess of the rainbow, down the multicolored bridge from Olympus to Crete to inform Menelaus of Helen's betrayal.

He could scarcely credit the news. Paris had been his guest. Would any man, especially one of royal blood, so abuse his host's hospitality? It was unthinkable. For a wife to flee her husband's walls was bad enough, but that a guest, and an honored one at that, should betray his host was beyond imagining.

In a fever of impatience Menelaus waited for the funeral games to be ended so that he could quit Crete and hurry home to see for himself. Sometimes the gods played tricks on mortals. Hera, he knew, was an avenging goddess. Perhaps all unknown

to himself he had offended her and she was punishing him
with this false alarm.

He found it hard to believe that Helen would desert him;
she had been a docile wife. It was true she was vain and extrav-
agant, but then she was beautiful beyond words to describe.
He had found pleasure in indulging her extravagances. It
never occurred to him that she might have been bored with
her life and with him. He thought back over the days since
the arrival of Paris at Sparta. Helen had been a charming
hostess, but nothing more than that. And Paris's behavior had
been all anyone could wish. He had been gallantly complimen-
tary to his lovely hostess, but in a way to flatter her husband.
Once Menelaus had caught open envy in his guest's eyes, and
his pride of possession had swelled in recognition of the glance.

And now they were gone together. Or so Iris had reported.
It couldn't be true. And how would he bear it if it was true?
He would be humiliated before the eyes of all Greece. A
man who couldn't command the loyalty of his own wife! He
thought of the oath. If Iris had spoken the truth, then Paris
and all Troy would suffer for this betrayal.

At last the games were ended and Menelaus and his company were free to depart. Though a strong south wind filled
their sail, it seemed to Menelaus that the ship sat glued to the
water. He paced the deck between the oarsmen, not daring to
let his anxiety show. To confide his fears even to his closest
counselor would make him a laughingstock if Helen was on
the palace wall to greet his return.

When they reached the mainland, the frantic husband
ordered his horses yoked at once even though night was approaching. At reckless speed in the darkness, his chariot cov-
ered the overland miles until his driver warned him of the
horses' exhaustion and they stopped to rest until dawn.

But no slender figure stood upon the walls as the chariot approached the palace from across the wide plain. In vain Menelaus's eyes swept the ramparts. Of course something may have kept her, he consoled himself. Yet this would be the first time she had failed to watch his approach from a long journey. As soon as the guardsman's quick eye spied the chariot rolling toward him, the word was taken at once to the queen and Helen would immediately take her stand high above the plain to welcome her lord.

An ominous silence greeted Menelaus as he entered his palace. Slaves scattered before him as if fearful of his presence. He hastened to the queen's apartment, entering without ceremony.

"Where is your mistress?" he demanded of a slave girl who knelt beside a brazier and looked up at him with frightened eyes. "Say at once, where is my wife?"

The slave girl crawled toward him, her head bent almost to the floor. All too often the bearer of bad news paid for it with his life.

In a small voice the girl said, "The queen is gone, my lord."

"Gone where?" demanded her master.

The girl sank lower onto the stone paving, almost prostrate before him. "I do not know, my lord."

Menelaus touched her with a foot, not too gently. "Fool, get up and tell me what you do know or it will go hard with you."

The girl scrambled to her feet. "I know only what I have been told," she whispered. "My mistress is gone and I am told that the prince from Troy has gone with her. They took much treasure with them. So I have been told."

Menelaus fixed her with such savage eyes that she cowered back as from a blow. But he wasn't seeing her, since he was

blind with rage. So it was all true what Iris had reported. He was a betrayed husband and a betrayed host.

For a moment he stood frozen; then, to the immense relief of the terrified slave girl, he spun on his heel and rushed from the apartment. Straight to the courtyard he went and ordered fresh horses yoked to his chariot.

His charioteer fixed him with sympathetic eyes. "Menelaus, I have heard, too. But it is useless to pursue them. They have been gone a long time."

"I do not plan to pursue them," returned his master. "We are going to Mycenae, to Agamemnon. The chiefs must be summoned and reminded of their oath. This means war."

His brother's wrath was only a little less savage than Menelaus's own. The House of Atreus had suffered insult. Paris and the city from which he sprang must make atonement.

"The time has come to fulfill the oath," declared Agamemnon. "We must summon the chiefs. I will send couriers to every kingdom demanding that each chief come with his ships and armed men to Aulis. When the ships are gathered, we will sail for Troy."

Aulis was at this time an important port city in Boeotia directly across a narrow strip of water from the long island known as Euboea. The gulf thus formed offered a safe anchor for a very large fleet.

Ships had already begun arriving at Aulis before Agamemnon's special courier arrived at distant stony Ithaca. But word of what was happening had already reached Odysseus, since word of mouth travels faster than the swiftest horse.

In the years since he had given old King Tyndareus sage advice, Odysseus had married a gentle maiden named Penelope.

Now he was the father of an infant son, Telemachus. He loved his wife and child. His herds were prospering. He was happy and secure. Now suddenly, disastrously, it seemed to him, he was about to be asked to fulfill an oath to save another man's pride. What did it matter to him that Paris had stolen Helen away from Menelaus? What difference did it make to him whether or not Menelaus got her back? What satisfaction would there be for him as an instrument of this return? And suppose their efforts proved futile? Troy was well fortified. This everyone knew. Suppose he were to meet death on the great plain before those formidable walls? Even though he died a hero's death, what comfort could this bring his wife and small son? And the war was sure to be a long one. How would Penelope fare without him? The more he thought about it, the more he hated this war in which he had no stake. Except for that foolish oath. How he wished he had never taken it! It had been madness, for never was there any hope that Helen could have been his. Happy in gentle Penelope's love, Odysseus wondered why he had ever aspired to Helen.

Yet as a man of honor, he must respect the oath he had sworn, however foolish. Was there a way to avoid the war and still not deny the oath? Odysseus put his clever mind to work.

On the very day the courier was to arrive at Ithaca, an idea came to him. He would feign madness! A madman would be a most unreliable ally. But first he must convince Penelope. If his own wife thought him mad, Agamemnon's courier would have to accept the fact. Steeling his heart, knowing he would deeply wound hers, Odysseus set about his deception.

When at the day's first meal Penelope greeted him with her customary affectionate smile, he glowered at her accusingly. His look erased her smile, and a troubled expression took its place.

"What is it, Odysseus? What has come over you that you look at me with angry eyes?" she asked.

"Do you expect me to eat this slop?" he yelled, and seizing a bowl from the table, hurled it at her.

"Dear love!" she cried and flung herself at his knees, grasping them in her arms. She looked up beseechingly into his furious face. "What madness has come upon you?"

For answer he toppled her with a kick and she lay helplessly sobbing, afraid to rise lest in his madness he do worse.

"Don't lie there blubbering. Get up and bring me food. Food I can eat!"

Slowly, painfully, Penelope rose and hastened from the room, her mind a turmoil. Had Hera sent this madness on Odysseus as once she had done to Heracles? But what harm had Odysseus done the goddess? What harm had he done to anyone? It was true he was wily and clever. But had this injured anyone? Never had he been anything but kind and loving to her, treating her always with the utmost courtesy and honor. Their marriage bed had been constructed in secret between them and one old servitor. One of its posts was a once living olive tree, and their bedroom had been designed around it. The branches had been cut away and the post richly carved. Now the tree was dead, but its roots still gripped the ground beneath the palace and prevented the bed's ever being moved. This he had done for love of her, and now this very morning he had abused her most shamefully and without cause. Surely Odysseus must be mad.

When Agamemnon's courier was announced, Odysseus refused to see him, ordering Penelope to receive him instead.

"My lady," began the courier, bowing respectfully before the wife of Odysseus, "I come from Agamemnon, king of Mycenae. He wishes to remind your husband of his oath to make war against the seducer of his brother's wife, Helen. Odysseus is to come with ships and men to Aulis, there to await the gathering of the full fleet for an assault on Troy. Should Odysseus ignore his oath, then his honor and perhaps his very life will be forfeit."

"Some dreadful curse has visited my husband," Penelope explained. "Only this morning a madness came upon him. Without warning and without cause he loosed a rage against me that gave me fear for my life. I am still trembling at the thought of it."

The courier looked hard at the young woman before him and saw that it was true. She was trembling from head to foot, and her cheeks were pale as death.

His voice was gentle when next he spoke to her. "You understand, madam, I cannot take that word back to Agamemnon on your statement alone. If Odysseus is truly mad, then, of course, his use to the Greek host is at an end. But I must see with my own eyes."

"I understand," said Penelope. "Remain here and I will try to persuade him to come to you."

But though she sought him throughout the palace, Odysseus was not to be found. She summoned a slave and bade him seek his master out-of-doors. "Don't return until you have found him," she commanded. "He cannot be far."

In a short while the slave was back with word that his master was plowing a field.

"But he has slaves for such work," protested Penelope.

"No slave would plow as he is," returned the man, a frightened look in his eyes.

"What do you mean?" demanded Penelope.

"My master must be mad. He has yoked an ass and an ox to his plow."

It was true then, thought Penelope, her beloved husband had become a madman.

She returned to the courier. "We must seek Odysseus in the fields," she told him. "He has taken on the work of a slave and you will see for yourself that he is mad."

The slave led the stranger out to where his master, wearing a peasant's hat, was plowing with his unlikely team. And as he marched along the furrow, Odysseus was flinging over his shoulder, as if sowing it behind him, pure salt. The evidence was plain. The man was mad.

The courier watched the strange scene, while Odysseus seemed not to know he was there. The stranger was almost convinced, yet a doubt lingered in his mind. He returned to the palace and requested another audience with Penelope.

"Before I go," he said, "may I see the son of this madman?"

For an instant some of her anxiety left Penelope's eyes. She was proud of little Telemachus. No mother could boast a finer child than he. Whatever terrible curse had been laid upon the father, there was no trace of it in the sturdy infant he had sired. She withdrew at once, returning quickly with the baby in her arms. The courier took him admiringly into his own arms, then, turning swiftly, raced with him out of the place to the field where Odysseus was still earnestly plowing and sowing his salt.

The courier approached the furrow, the child in his arms. He waited until the team was about ten yards from him; then, stooping, he gently laid the baby exactly in the path of the approaching team. He stood back and waited.

On they came, the ox and the ass, closer and closer to the cooing Telemachus, who was waving his hands and feet at the sky, quite unmindful of the approaching danger. Now the team was very near and the courier tensed to snatch the child before the first hoof could touch him. But even as he readied himself, the driver jerked the team to one side and the plow slid harmlessly past the still unknowing baby.

"So, Odysseus, you thought to fool me. Your ruse almost worked. Now I remind you of your oath. Make haste to gather what ships you can and join the fleet at Aulis. Agamemnon will be glad of your support."

So saying, the courier turned on his heel and departed from Odysseus and his palace.

By this time Penelope and her women had arrived on the scene, all frantic over the child's abduction. Penelope snatched him from the ground and felt him over carefully. The baby laughed at what he thought was playful tickling.

"Is the courier mad, too, that he should want to sacrifice this child to your madness?" she cried.

In answer, Odysseus reached out and drew her to him.

"No, my love," he comforted her. "It is only that he is wilier than I. I had sought to avoid leaving you and our son, but the fates are against us. Be prepared for a long widowhood, Penelope. It has been foretold that if I leave for Troy I will not return to my homeland for twenty years."

She wept with mingled joy and dread. At least her dear Odysseus had been returned to her. But only to be snatched away again. She vowed she would be faithful; she would be patient. And someday, she felt sure, despite the dreadful prophecy, he would return to her.

It had been foretold that the Trojan War could not be won without the aid of Achilles. Though he was far too young to have sued for Helen's hand and thus was not bound by the oath, he was now a youth somewhere under twenty, and of fighting age and trim.

However, Thetis, his mother, by her own gift of prophecy,

knew he would not return alive from the fighting at Troy, and she was determined to save him from his fate. To this end, she arranged with Lycomedes, king of the island of Scyros, to allow him to live with his daughters disguised as a girl. Achilles, then about ten years old, was removed from the guardianship of the good centaur, Cheiron, and taken to the distant island. Dressed in a princess's raiment, his long blond locks, finely chiseled features, and slender body made him indistinguishable from the girls around him. They were soon in on the secret, though, and when he had grown to adolescence one of them fell in love with this "sister" and had a child by him.

Now with the ships arriving each day at the port of Aulis and preparations for the war going forward, it was necessary to find Achilles without further delay. Only no one knew where he was.

As usual in any dilemma stemming out of the war, Odysseus's counsel was sought.

"I do not know where Achilles is, either," confessed Odysseus, "but the other night I had a dream."

No one appeared bored by this announcement, for well they knew that dreams were portents. Agamemnon and the chiefs about him waited respectfully for Odysseus to continue.

"In this dream I appeared as a peddler at the court of a king who had fathered many daughters."

Agamemnon sighed. "What king has not?" he asked, glancing around at the others with a wry smile.

Odysseus caught the smile and observed, "None so comely as your Iphigenia, Agamemnon."

The great king smiled. "She is one among thousands, my Iphigenia. The delight of my heart, a credit to her lady mother and a joy to all around her. But go on, Odysseus. What of this king's many daughters?"

"One among them was not a daughter, though dressed as a

girl. In my dream I was fooled at first, accepting him as one of the princesses. Then something in his stride alerted me to the truth. On looking closer, I noticed a muscling in the chest and arm that not even Athena could attain to. At that moment I awoke."

"Before the location of the palace was revealed, I suppose," Menelaus remarked dryly. He had been staying at Mycenae since his discovery of Helen's flight.

Odysseus shrugged. " 'Twas but a dream," he reminded them.

"Still it bears thinking on," declared Agamemnon. "Put your good mind to work, Odysseus."

Odysseus did. The ancestry of Achilles was well known. It was also known that he was to have a short life and a glorious one. Now suppose, Odysseus speculated, a goddess-mother (and the mother of Achilles was a sea nymph) wanted to shield her young son from a war which meant certain death to him. What better could she do than disguise his sex and hide him far from the focal point of that war? Odysseus smiled to himself and nodded wisely. He thought he had the answer to his question.

The very next day, accompanied by Diomedes, both disguised as peddlers, Odysseus departed from Mycanae with a peddler's horde sure to delight a young lady's heart. Odysseus had already applied his knowledge and that of others to the problem of Achilles and had come to the conclusion that Lycomedes, king of Scyros, best met the elements of his dream and suspicions.

It began as another boring day in the palace at Scyros. While the princesses busied themselves at their weaving and embroidery, Achilles sat glumly, chin in hand, staring hopelessly before him. Though he had early on been schooled in these same domestic accomplishments, he had now, at age sixteen, refused to cooperate any longer in this ridiculous charade. When would he again be allowed to practice the manly arts that Cheiron had taught him? His mother had warned him that he was not to disclose his identity until a sign was given him. If he did, there would be terrible consequences. He could not imagine anything worse for him than the life he was at present living, but his mother was a goddess and he dared not go against her will.

His mood was interrupted by the sudden entrance of a slave announcing that two peddlers had arrived at the palace and were displaying their wares on the porch for the princesses' approval. The girls, twittering happily, quickly abandoned their tasks and with something less than royal dignity hastened from the room. Still Achilles sat, indifferent. At the door one of them paused to look back at him.

"Come, Achilles. Why sit glum and glowering? These peddlers have come from afar, surely. They may have tales to tell. Why not come and hear them?"

The youth hauled himself out of his chair with a studied lack of eagerness. "You may be right," he said grudgingly. "Anything for diversion in this backwater." The girl gave him a quick smile and sped after her sisters. Achilles sauntered slowly behind her.

Odysseus eyed them closely as the girls emerged from the palace onto the columned porch. Which one among them might be Achilles? It was impossible to tell; they looked much alike. While they were bending excitedly over his wares, Odysseus studied them as best he could. But they moved about quickly, exclaiming and holding up lengths of silk and chains of Egyptian gold.

The wily Odysseus had prepared for just such a predicament. Underneath all the silks and gowns and embroideries he had hidden a sword, and with it a bronze shield.

So attentively was his gaze upon the princesses that he never noticed when a late arrival came upon the porch and leaned indifferently against a marble column.

When the girls had rifled the rich horde to the point where the weapons lay revealed, Odysseus gave a signal to Diomedes standing some paces off. Instantly a trumpet blast sounded forth. The girls shrieked in alarm. The palace was under attack! They fled the porch in a body. All but one. At the trumpet's alarm, reacting instinctively to the summons, this "princess" ripped the gown from her shoulders and, seizing the sword and shield, braced herself for battle. In that moment Cheiron could have been proud of his pupil.

Odysseus laughed and laid an affectionate hand on the youth's shoulder. "So we have found you, Achilles."

Achilles stepped back, shrugging off the hand.

"Insolent peddler, lay no hand on me. What can Achilles mean to you?"

"I know it to be a name that will ring with glory down the ages," replied Odysseus. "Men will thrill to its accents as they will to the heroic deeds for which it stands."

Somewhat mollified by these flattering words, Achilles lowered the sword and looked less fiercely at the peddler.

"Who are you?" he asked. "And why have you come here?"

"I am Odysseus of Ithaca, and this"—he turned to summon Diomedes to his side—"is Diomedes of Argos, who has eighty ships waiting at Aulis for the attack on Troy."

Achilles' face lit with sudden joy. This was the sign his mother had told him of. These men had come to summon him to join the war. Now his life of glory could begin, for, of course, he would go with them. He would need weapons; he would need horses; he would need ships. His father, Peleus, would provide them. Nothing must stand in his way now. Troy was his destiny.

Peleus not only fitted out his son with weapons, but made him a gift of his team of immortal horses, a wedding gift from Poseidon. The horses were twin foals, golden in color, and one of them, Xanthus, had the power of speech. Thetis contributed a suit of armor, the work of Hephaestus, god of the forge.

Achilles was also given a fleet of fifty ships, representing the contribution to the war of several provinces. He was also, though so very young, made admiral of the fleet assembled at Aulis. Agamemnon, who had brought a hundred ships, was named leader of the Greek host.

THE SACRIFICE
OF IPHIGENIA

A thousand ships lay in the harbor of Aulis. Some were drawn up on the beach. Others, held by stone anchors, floated in the shallower waters of the bay. All were becalmed.

Men, slaves, sailors, warriors swarmed about the city, bored with their inaction as they waited for a favorable wind to drive their ships to Troy. There was mutiny in the air.

The fault was Agamemnon's. While waiting for a fair wind, he had gone hunting with some of his Argives and had shot a hind. It happened to be a favorite hind of Artemis's, and he compounded the injury by declaring as the animal fell, "Not even Artemis could have shot better than that!" Of course the goddess heard him and was doubly furious. To punish his rash act and boast, Artemis withheld the wind that would blow the fleet to Troy.

Day after day the calm held. No breeze moved the leaves on any tree; no bird sang. Even the sea was hushed and quiet. All the world seemed to be holding its breath while the ships lay motionless upon the water.

Some of the Greeks were for returning home.

"Why do we dawdle about in this place, wasting our time and fortunes, supporting slaves and fighters who sit idly day after day, while at home our fields and flocks need our husbanding?" they asked one another. "For what purpose do we idle here? So that Agamemnon can strut in his command of a thousand ships? Or that Menelaus may get his wife back? What has that to do with us?"

Such talk frightened Agamemnon. He enjoyed his position as leader of this host. No one had ever commanded anything like it. To have it all peter out now, before even a ship could sail, was a most ignominious outcome of what had promised to be a heroic venture. All his life he had longed for glory, and had seen this assault on Troy as a means of obtaining it. Now such glory was about to be snatched from him all because a needed wind refused to blow. *Why* wouldn't it blow? What dark powers were balking him? He would ask Calchas. The seer would know. He should have summoned him before.

Calchas had joined the Greek host at the express urging of Agamemnon, who knew it would be useful to have so fine a seer with them. He it was who had predicted that the war against Troy could not be won without Achilles. And only within the last few days he had predicted how long it would last.

Agamemnon had been sacrificing to Zeus and Apollo when a serpent with blood-red markings on its back slid from under the altar, glided straight to a tree outside the temple, climbed it, and in view of everyone devoured the eight baby sparrows nesting there, along with their mother. This, declared Calchas, meant that the war would be fought for nine years and that in the tenth year Troy would fall.

So now Agamemnon had called the seer to his tent to explain, in the presence of Menelaus and Odysseus, why they were becalmed.

"The fault lies with you, Agamemnon," Calchas said. "You killed a favorite hind of Artemis and boasted of your kill. For this she has becalmed you as punishment. Only you can appease her."

"How?" demanded Agamemnon.

"You must sacrifice your daughter, Iphigenia, to Artemis. Only by her death will the goddess allow the fleet to sail to Troy."

Agamemnon sat fingering his beard. It never occurred to him to question the seer's advice. He accepted that he must choose between Iphigenia's life and his own glory. It was a hard choice, and Agamemnon began to rationalize his decision, for, of course, Iphigenia, much as he loved her, must die. He could not go back on the Greeks gathered here, he reasoned. They had come at his summons to save the pride of his house. He would be disgraced if he abandoned them now merely to save a daughter's life. And Troy must be punished. A prince of Troy had grossly injured the king of Sparta. That injury must be avenged.

Slowly Agamemnon rose to his feet. Not one man had spoken since Calchas had uttered his dreadful pronouncement. All eyes were on their leader as they waited for his next words.

"If Troy can be won only at the cost of my daughter's life, then I must pay the price. No greater sacrifice could be asked, for she is dear as life to me. Let no word of this escape among the ships. No rumor must reach Mycenae of the girl's fate. Only we four must know."

The three departed and Agamemnon faced alone the task of getting Iphigenia to Aulis. He could not just send for her. This was a war camp. Her mother would wonder at the impropriety of having a young girl brought to such a spot.

Clytemnestra might well refuse to let the child leave home. What ruse could he use to get her here? Suddenly he had it, and something like a smile of satisfaction settled around his mouth. He drew his writing materials toward him and began a letter to his wife.

Mycenae, too, seemed becalmed with its king and gallant warriors gone. To be sure, a decent company had been left behind to guard the palace, and slaves went as usual about their daily work. But the pulsing heart of its activity, Agamemnon, was absent, and there had settled upon the community behind the great Cyclopean walls a kind of inertia that would endure for long.

It was, therefore, a welcome diversion for Clytemnestra when a messenger was shown into the queen's presence with a letter from her husband. It must be something of grave import, she assumed as she took the tablet into her hands. Aulis was a long way from Mycenae. He would hardly be sending back for an extra horse or spear! Then another thought flashed through her mind. Why had the ships not yet sailed? They should have been halfway to Troy by this time.

She broke the seal on the tablet and began to read. A sharp intake of breath was all that revealed her emotion as she read. Her face gave no hint of what the letter contained, good news or bad. When she had finished reading, she directed that the messenger be fed and bathed and that he await her future pleasure. Next she sent for Iphigenia.

She came promptly to her mother's apartment, pausing respectfully just inside the door.

"Come here, child," said Clytemnestra, putting out her hand. "I have wondrous news for you."

Iphigenia came forward quickly. She was a pretty young

thing, slim and sweet and gentle-eyed. An affectionate smile curved her lips as she approached her mother. She knelt beside Clytemnestra and stretched her slender arms across her mother's lap. Her eyes, expectant, were raised to meet the older woman's downward glance.

"I have here a letter from your father. He has summoned us to Aulis. Can you imagine why?"

Iphigenia shook her head, her smile fading. "To Aulis? Why would he summon us to an armed camp?"

"For the best reason in the world, my daughter. You are to be married to the great Achilles."

Iphigenia withdrew her arms and sank back upon her heels. "Achilles!" she breathed. "Is it possible?"

"Not only possible; it is all but accomplished."

The girl looked bewildered. "But will not Achilles accompany the fleet to Troy?"

"Most assuredly," replied Clytemnestra.

"Then why should he wish to marry so precipitately on the very eve of his departure? It has been foretold that the war will be a long one. It may be years before he can see his wife again."

Clytemnestra smiled tolerantly and put an arm around the girl's slim shoulders.

"Dear innocent, you do not understand these things. It is as well you don't, for you are a proper maiden, gently reared. Achilles, like any man going into danger, will face it more happily knowing he has left an heir behind him. He has chosen you to be the mother of that heir. It does you honor, Iphigenia."

The girl, blushing, hid her face in her mother's lap. Her voice came muffled. "Will he love me?"

Clytemnestra came as near to a snort as her dignity would

allow. "What nonsense is this? He will love you well enough
if you give him a son. Make ready. We leave for Aulis tomor-
row at the first light."

Iphigenia rose to her feet and quietly withdrew. Her mother's word was law; a daughter had no say in her own destiny.
Already Achilles was considered great, she told herself. Troy
could not be taken without him. Doubtless he would be
greater as the war continued. Perhaps the greatest man among
all the Greek warriors. She would be honored as his wife. Still,
would he love her? As she went about her preparations for the
long journey to Aulis, she decided to offer up some prayers to
Aphrodite before leaving home.

Agamemnon's messenger had been gone a day on the route
to Mycenae when the king began to have second thoughts
about the sacrifice of his daughter. As much as a father could
love a girl child, he loved Iphigenia. From birth she had been
his pet, his plaything. He admired her quick intelligence, her
gentle beauty. Above all, he cherished her evident fondness
for him. She dared liberties with him neither of her sisters
would have dared. He thought now of those sisters. Either one
of them he could have sacrificed to Artemis with only slight
qualms, especially Electra, whose dark brooding beauty was
so like her mother's. Why had the goddess insisted on having
Iphigenia? What had he really done to deserve such excruciat-
ing punishment? He would defy the goddess. He would save
this beloved child and his own conscience.

As he wrestled with his conscience, Agamemnon's whole
demeanor registered his inward struggle. He became sleepless,
pacing before his tent in the moonlight. He was irritable to
those around him. He would give out orders impulsively, only

to rescind them later. In short, he was not himself, and his brother, Menelaus, took sudden note of the fact.

All along, Menelaus had been fearful that his brother would waver in his decision to sacrifice Iphigenia. He knew well how fond Agamemnon was of the girl; he, too, had a daughter of whom he was fond. So each day he had appeared in Agamemnon's tent, applauding his courage and manliness for having made such a hard decision. Nor did he fail to emphasize the stature Agamemnon had gained as leader of this great fighting force.

His anxiety regarding the expedition was scarcely disinterested! Should Agamemnon go back on his agreement to sacrifice his daughter in exchange for a fair wind for Troy, there was no hope that Helen would ever be returned to him and her paramour punished.

Thus it was that Menelaus was in the vicinity of the leader's tent when an aged and trusted slave of Agamemnon's slipped into it one moonlit night.

The king sat in the shadowy and smoky light of an oil-burning lamp.

"Why have you sent for me, my lord Agamemnon? The hour is late. Should you not be on your couch asleep?"

"Sleep avoids me, old man. I have had much on my mind of late."

" 'Twould seem so. I have watched you and have seen you pacing restlessly up and down before your tent. What eats at your heart, my lord?"

The old man approached the table and stood looking at what lay upon it. It was plain he was a privileged slave. "I see you have been writing a letter, Agamemnon. Tell me what prompts this letter. You know you can trust me, for I came with your bride, Clytemnestra, when she left her father's house for yours. For many long years I have been your trusted servant. You know I am honest. You can unburden your heart to me, O, King."

"Well spoken, old man. Hear then a king's confidences. Some days ago the seer, Calchas, prophesied that we cannot expect a fair wind for Troy unless I sacrifice to angry Artemis my daughter Iphigenia. At the time I agreed to this, though with a heavy heart. But the decision has caused me such suffering that I can no longer bear it. In the letter you see lying here, I have rescinded the one already sent to Clytemnestra, urging her to bring our daughter hither. In it I even said that she was to marry Achilles, though he knows nothing about it, nor has he ever sued for her hand. It was an excuse to get her here, for never would her mother have brought her otherwise."

"Who knows about your promise to sacrifice your daughter?" asked the old servant.

"Only Menelaus and Odysseus besides Calchas and myself."

Agamemnon picked up the tablet and handed it to the slave. "Get to Mycenae with all speed. Let your legs recall their youth and do not dally in the forest shade. Look well at every crossroads that the ladies' carriage does not pass you, for they may already have started. If so, turn them back. If necessary, seize the horses' bridles in your hands and turn the carriage around."

The old man put the tablet into the pouch he wore at his belt. "Suppose I do come upon the ladies traveling in this direction. How will they know that this second letter comes from your hand?"

"They will know by this," said Agamemnon and slipped from a finger of his right hand a gold ring bearing a seal. "Here, take it and guard it well. By this the queen will know that your message is authentic." He watched the slave carefully place the ring deep in the pouch. "Go now," he told him. "And may Hermes, god of travelers, speed you on your way."

The old man bowed and, parting the tent flaps, slipped into the darkness beyond.

He had not gone far when an arm came brutally around his throat and he was yanked backward off his feet. At the same time he felt the pouch wrenched off his belt. Released after a brief struggle, he was amazed to see Menelaus in the moonlight before him.

"Why are you sneaking through the camp at this ungodly hour, old man? What errand is so urgent that Agamemnon cannot wait for dawn? I think I know."

"You have no right to take my pouch." Menelaus was already drawing from it the letter to Clytemnestra. The old man made a grab for it, but Menelaus held it out of reach. "You have no right to read my lord's letter."

For answer, Menelaus moved out of the shadow to where the moonlight fell full upon the tablet. He broke the seal and perused it quickly. "So, it is even as I surmised. My brother's courage has deserted him. He would betray the expedition. But first he shall hear from me."

The old man did not stay to hear his words. Already he was hurrying to Agamemnon's tent to inform his master of his brother's treachery.

He entered the tent without ceremony to find Agamemnon asleep at the table, his head resting on his folded arms. It was as if, his decision made and Iphigenia saved, all strength had gone out of him and his long-delayed slumber had taken possession of his tortured mind.

"Agamemnon! My lord, awaken."

The king jerked awake.

"Your brother, Menelaus, waylaid me and seized your letter."

At that moment Menelaus entered the tent. He rudely shoved the old man to one side. "What he says is true. Get rid of him. I have something to say to you, my brother."

At a signal from Agamemnon, the old man withdrew.

"How dare you intercept a message of mine or lay hands upon my messenger?" Agamemnon had risen and now faced his brother, his face dark with fury.

"What right had you to send such a message?" Menelaus shot back, not flinching under the other's furious eyes. "This letter is treason. The Greeks shall know the kind of leader they have chosen, for I intend to show it to all the camp."

"Give it to me," said Agamemnon, putting out his hand.

"Not until I have shown it to all the chiefs."

"How came you upon the old man?" demanded Agamemnon. "How long have you been spying on me? Menelaus, you are shameless."

"I was watching to see if the ladies had arrived yet from Mycenae."

"A likely tale," scoffed Agamemnon. "The lies come glibly to your tongue. My ladies are my own business."

"All right then," returned Menelaus, "I lingered outside your tent because it pleased me to do so. I am not your slave, brother."

"Nor am I yours. And I now order you, Menelaus, to stay away from this tent unless I summon you to it."

"Before I go, there are some questions I want to put to you, Agamemnon. Do you remember how anxious you were to have the command of this host? Do you recall how you let everyone think you were indifferent to such an honor? How humble you were! Offering your hand to the least among the warriors, inviting the lowly to your door. Your ears were alert and sympathetic to anyone's problems. You were solicitous to the chiefs, accessible to them at all hours. No difficulty was too slight to merit your attention. Do you remember all this? And so they gave the power into your hands."

"I brought the most ships," protested Agamemnon. "I brought a hundred ships. That is why they made me their leader."

"I admit it had something to do with it," Menelaus agreed. "But it was your attitude that confirmed it. Agamemnon, friend of every man. A leader who would be approachable, who would consider the good of all, irrespective of rank. And then what happened? No sooner had you gained the power than your attitude changed. You became haughty and overbearing. You no longer recognized on the street men whose hands you had clasped. A good man does not abandon his old friends when he has won new honors, Agamemnon. Rather he looks upon them as a valuable part of the past that has formed him. No man is self-made. A successful man is the result of every person who has touched his life.

"Then you arrived at Aulis, and suddenly you were nothing. Not all your blustering and posturing could make a fair wind blow. The days passed and then the weeks. There was muttering among the chiefs. Idle sailors grew insolent; violent quarrels broke out among the fighting men. Some were for returning home. You could see your command dissolving before your eyes. Great Agamemnon might have to return to Mycenae like a dog with its tail between its legs. So you called in Calchas and he told you what you must do. You were glad of his advice. Don't deny it. You saw a way to save yourself and with small reluctance sent for Clytemnestra and your daughter.

"Now you sing a different tune. What kind of leader is he who gives a command one moment and recalls it the next? How Troy would rejoice to know we had such a leader! Now will all the world know that Priam and his infamous rutting son can shame the House of Atreus with impunity. I am disgraced to have a brother like you, Agamemnon."

With his final word, Menelaus turned away and started toward the opening in the tent.

"Wait," said Agamemnon, coming from around the table. "I have listened to you. Now it is your turn to listen to me. I am still your commander, and I order you to stay and hear me."

His eyes contemptuous, Menelaus turned slowly around to face his brother.

"I shall speak reasonably to you, Menelaus, as brothers should. Why do you upbraid me? What is your stake in this expedition? I can answer that. It is to have returned to your arms a wife without virtue. Why should good men risk their lives, why should my daughter's life be sacrificed for the sake of Helen? It is true that caught up in the first anger at the insult Paris did to you and to our House, I thought one way. Now, after due consideration, I think another. What is wrong with that? A man can change his mind, and I will not kill my child. For the rest of my life the horror of it would live with me. It is folly to make war for such a silly cause as yours. These men, mad with longing for Helen, swore a foolish oath. All Greece must be mad. Well, I am no longer mad. I have come to my senses, Menelaus. It is time you came to yours."

He had hardly finished speaking when a messenger burst into the tent. "My lord, Agamemnon, your daughter and her queen mother are here. And your little son, Orestes. Even now they have halted by the spring in the meadow and are bathing their feet and watering their tired horses. Your heart may rejoice for it is long since you have seen them. Crowds have gone to the meadow to gaze upon them, and men wonder why you have summoned them here. Is it for a marriage? Shall we prepare for a sacrifice? Tell me, that I may take the word and prepare a proper celebration for this occasion."

"Your news is most welcome," said Agamemnon, his voice steady. "As for the rest, it must await my pleasure. Go now."

The messenger sped off and Agamemnon whirled about, a hand to his face. For a moment his bent shoulders shook, and when he turned back to Menelaus, tears were streaming down his cheeks.

"What dreadful Fate pursues me? These tears shame me, Menelaus, but I am powerless to prevent them. What am I to tell Clytemnestra? She has come here all trusting to give her daughter in marriage. And what shall I tell my child, whose life the Fates will claim? How shall I greet them, what can I say to them? Disaster is upon me."

These anguished words, torn from his heart together with his brother's bitter tears, had an instant effect upon Menelaus. Rage and contempt left his face, and he moved toward his brother, all compassion.

"Forgive me, Agamemnon. I withdraw the words I just spoke to you. Here, let me take your hand and comfort you. We are both sons of Atreus. A brother is more important to me than a wife. Why should your child die because of Helen? Indeed, she shall not. Let the ships return to their home places. Let us go back to Mycenae. Let us forget it all and let Iphigenia live."

"I welcome your words, Menelaus. Brothers should not quarrel. But it is too late to save Iphigenia now she is here."

"Why too late?" demanded Menelaus, now as eager to save the girl as before he had been to sacrifice her.

"The assembled armies will demand her death in exchange for a fair wind for Troy. They hunger for this war. They see glory and tribute at the end of it. They are fired with fighting spirit. They will kill her and you and me in order to conquer Troy."

Agamemnon took his brother's hand, his face heavy with sorrow. "I am grateful for your comfort, my brother, but there is no possible way that Iphigenia can now be saved."

"Why not?" demanded Menelaus. "You are her father; her fate lies in your hands."

Agamemnon shook his head. "The whole Greek host will demand her life. And if we oppose it, ours as well."

"Surely not if you send her home again."

"They all know that she is here. Soon they will know the reason. Calchas will proclaim the prophecy."

"Not if we kill him first," suggested Menelaus.

"Odysseus knows the prophecy. Even if Calchas were dead, he would let it out. It's true he came here against his will, but now he is as keen for this war as the most bloodthirsty. Thus does the atmosphere of a war camp and the talk of fighting men influence all. He knows the mob. And he is cunning. He will know how to incite them against me if I refuse to make the sacrifice. This camp is now in such a mood that these men would follow us to Mycenae if we slipped away, and there raze the Cyclopean walls and lay waste the kingdom."

Agamemnon's words ceased, and for a moment there was silence within the tent. Then he spoke again.

"There is one thing you can do for me, Menelaus. See to it that Clytemnestra knows nothing of my plan. Let her think anything she wants until I have taken the child and sacrificed her."

"I will do what I can," said Menelaus and left the tent.

By this time the women from Mycenae had quit the meadow and were approaching the large tent which had been readied for their use. Attendants were rushing forward to help them down from the carriage. Clytemnestra held the toddler, Orestes. Though she knew a child so young could only be a nuisance on such a long journey, still she dared not leave him at home. He was Agamemnon's sole heir, and with the king gone, some petty chieftain, seeing this as an opportunity to augment his own power, might well attack Mycenae. If successful, the first thing he would do would be to slaughter the little prince. So now she handed the young child over the carriage wheels to the arms of a stalwart slave who received him gladly. Next the queen, herself, was carefully handed down, and after her, Iphigenia.

They paused at the entrance to the tent and Clytemnestra turned to her daughter. "Stay close to me. We have been courteously received, but this is a camp of war, and rough men are about. Until your father comes . . ." She checked herself as Agamemnon appeared in the distance. "Here he is now. Run and greet him."

Iphigenia sped off and threw herself into her father's arms. "It's been so long since I saw you," she said against his chest as he held her close, his head bowed above her. She lifted her head and smiled up at him. "I am so happy to see you."

"I, too, little one, am happy to see you."

They walked to where Clytemnestra awaited them.

"We are here, Agamemnon, at your bidding," she said, bowing formally to him.

"You have done well to come as I directed."

Clytemnestra smiled. "And for a happy purpose."

"Yes," cried Iphigenia, "most happy for us all. And yet, Father, your eyes are somber. A frown sits on your brow. Let me smooth it away," and she reached up playfully and smoothed the skin between his shaggy brows, laughing happily.

"You are too young to understand the cares I have," said Agamemnon, the frown back in place. "I am both general and king, and my cares are endless."

"Well, forget them now that we are here," she replied with the easy optimism of youth. "You can go back to your worries after I am gone."

"After you are gone," he repeated, and tears flooded his eyes.

"Why these sudden tears, my father? I don't understand. Surely there is no reason for sorrow except that you are going on a long voyage. You will go away from me. It is I who should be weeping, but my joy at being with you is too great. Oh, let us be joyful together while we can," she urged.

But no lightening of his sorrow appeared in Agamemnon's face. "You, too, are destined for a long voyage, my daughter."

Iphigenia flung her arms around him in sudden joy. "You mean I am to go with you, Father? Will my mother come, too?"

"No," said Agamemnon, shaking his head sadly. "For this voyage you must go alone."

"Am I going then to a new home?" she asked, blushing slightly, for her marriage to Achilles would mean her traveling north to Thessaly.

Again Agamemnon shook his head. "In a sense a new home," he said.

Iphigenia drew back, pouting. "You talk in riddles. But

when you have done in Troy what you have to do, then hurry back to me."

"First I must make sacrifice," her father informed her.

"Oh, yes, that is only proper," said Iphigenia.

"And you will be there," said Agamemnon.

"Then should I not start the dance around the altar?"

"No, for the present go into the tent and remain there with your maidens. Kiss me now, for soon we shall part, and it will be a long parting."

Again Iphigenia rushed into his arms, and he held her close. Then he turned her around and with a gentle push started her toward the entrance to the tent.

All this while Clytemnestra had been standing quietly by, watching the affectionate play between her husband and this favorite child of them both. But as their conversation went on, a puzzled look had settled on the queen's face. Agamemnon had noted it, and now he turned to her with an air of apology.

"Forgive me, Clytemnestra, for my seeming weakness. When I think that our beloved daughter is so soon to go to another's house, it saddens me. Achilles will make her a good husband, but her marriage means her going from our home forever."

"I understand your grief and even share it," returned Clytemnestra. "Yet marriage is the true destiny of young girls and this is a good marriage for our Iphigenia. Or so I believe. Tell me more about this young hero."

Relieved to have the subject changed, Agamemnon enlarged upon the virtues of Achilles, his semi-divine heritage, his rearing by Cheiron, his fleetness of foot, his prowess at arms, his good looks and honored position among the fighting men.

"Have you made arrangements for the marriage?" asked Clytemnestra.

"Everything is in readiness. It will take place when the moon is full to bring them good luck."

"And the sacrifices," continued the queen. "What sacrifice have you arranged for Artemis?"

"It is arranged for," answered Agamemnon bitterly. "One more thing. I know you have come here, Clytemnestra, to give our daughter away as is the custom. But for this marriage I intend to give away the bride."

Clytemnestra gasped in astonishment. *"You!"* she exclaimed. "It is most improper, and what, meanwhile, am I supposed to be doing?"

"You are to return immediately to Mycenae, leaving Iphigenia here with her father and her betrothed."

"This is an outrage." Clytemnestra's brooding face was inflamed with fury. "Why do you insult me thus?"

"Obey me," thundered Agamemnon in a furious voice. "You must return home to protect our other daughters. It is not seemly that they should be left so long alone."

"They are safe enough in their maiden quarters," Clytemnestra informed him. "You may say what you please and do what you please, but I shall stay here and see that this marriage is fittingly performed."

On these defiant words, Clytemnestra turned from her husband and entered the tent.

"What a fool a man is to let his wife leave home," Agamemnon muttered. "He should keep her at all times within his walls or else remain single. Now I must go and find Calchas and hurry up this sacrifice or all Greece will be in turmoil."

He hurried off, and Clytemnestra emerged from the tent and watched him disappearing among the armed men. What mischief was he up to now, she wondered, and why was he so anxious to get her out of Aulis?

Suddenly her eye was caught by a warrior striding toward her. He was young and very handsome. He paused to speak to one of Agamemnon's aides.

"Where is Agamemnon?" he demanded. "Where is the commander-in-chief? Tell him Achilles wants to see him. I cannot longer control my fighting men. They are as weary as I of waiting here useless because no wind blows. They are all for returning home." His eye caught Clytemnestra as she stepped away from her tent.

"Greetings, Achilles, son of Thetis," she said.

Achilles bowed. "Gracious lady and most beautiful, who are you that greets me so courteously?"

"I am Clytemnestra, wife to Agamemnon."

"Is it possible?" breathed Achilles. "And what is a lady doing in a camp of armed men? It is not seemly that I should be here speaking alone with you."

Bowing again quickly, he turned to go.

Clytemnestra smiled. "Nay, the circumstances are different for us." She put out her hand to him. "Take my hand in recognition of a welcome betrothal."

Achilles stood aghast. "I do not know what you mean, Clytemnestra. What marriage do you speak of?"

Clytemnestra smiled again, tolerantly. "It is but natural for young men to be shy on such an occasion as this. Of course I refer to your marriage with my daughter, Iphigenia."

"Lady, forgive me, I mean no insult. But surely your mind must be deranged to have put such words in your mouth."

Bewilderment settled on the queen's face. "Now it is I who do not understand you."

"I can only tell you that never have I courted your daughter, nor do I know of any marriage plans between us. We must talk this over and find out where the truth lies."

Clytemnestra stepped back. "Oh, I have been most terribly deceived," she cried. "The betrothal was a trick to get us here. Oh, I am humiliated before you! But why, why would Agamemnon so shame us both?"

"Perhaps it is some misunderstanding." Achilles comforted her. "Be sure, Queen Clytemnestra, you are no less honored in my sight because of it. I, too, feel injured. But let us not worry about it. I shall find Agamemnon and demand an explanation."

All at once a voice came from the leader's tent: "Wait. I am but a slave, yet I can make everything clear to you."

The old man to whom Agamemnon had confided his second letter emerged from the tent and threw himself at Clytemnestra's feet. "You know me, my lady. I was a gift to you from your father Tyndareus. I belong to you, and I feel greater loyalty to you than to your husband."

"Out with it. What do you know that we should know?" demanded Clytemnestra.

"That her father intends to kill your daughter. He intends to offer her as a sacrifice to Artemis in exchange for a fair wind for Troy."

Clytemnestra's face was ashen. "How do you know this, old man?"

As quickly as possible the old slave told of the night when Agamemnon had given him the second letter and why it was so necessary to speed to Mycenae in order to waylay the departure of the queen and her daughter.

"He meant to save his child, but Menelaus tore the letter from my hand and forced the king to carry out Calchas's prophecy."

"And the marriage—that was a trick to bring her here." Clytemnestra's face and voice were full of hate.

The old man nodded.

Clytemnestra began to weep, and all her queenly bearing forsook her. She was a mother, any mother, suffering for her child. Moved by her distress, Achilles took a step toward her. Instantly the once-proud queen was on her knees before him.

"Behold me here, a woman most miserable. I am mortal only, and you are half divine. Use then that power to save me and my daughter. Save her life and save me from great anguish. In all good faith I brought Iphigenia here to be your bride. It was your name that brought us here. Help us and prevent this smirch upon your name. Without your help we are lost."

"Your words do me honor," Achilles answered her. "And I swear I shall do what I can to save this girl. I now consider her my true betrothed and I will kill any man who dares to lay a hand upon her, though that man be her father. If through me your daughter should die, then I would be forever shamed. But she shall not die. Besides, Agamemnon has done me great injury. Behind my back and without my knowledge he pledged me in marriage to his daughter. He used my name without my consent. He shall answer for that. If he wanted to use my name, he should have asked leave of me." For a moment he considered. "Who knows, perhaps to save the expedition I might have agreed to his deceiving you." Then he flung up his head, and his eyes were angry. "But now it is different. If he tries to take his daughter from me now, I will fight him for her. I shall have her as my wife at whatever cost."

"May Heaven reward you for your help to us, Achilles. Do you wish now to see my daughter? It would be more seemly if she remained within our tent, but if you wish to have her add her pleas to mine, I will summon her here."

Achilles shook his head. "No, do not bring her before me.

Let us avoid any scandal." He moved a step closer to the queen. "Listen to me well, Clytemnestra. I think it is still possible to persuade your husband away from his foul plan. Reason can accomplish more than violence, and we will thus avoid involving the whole camp in the dread matter."

"I have little hope of persuading him, yet I will try," Clytemnestra promised. "Where shall I find you after I have spoken to him?"

"I will look for you," said Achilles. "I don't want you seeking me through the camp. That would be unbecoming to your dignity." He took quick leave of her.

Clytemnestra, knowing what her painful duty was, went into her own tent to inform Iphigenia of the destiny awaiting her.

It was hard at first for the mother to convince the child that her father actually intended to kill her.

"But he loves me as I love him," she protested wildly. "What madness has come upon him that he wishes my death?"

"Greed for power prompted him first," explained her mother. "In fairness you must know that he attempted to rescind the order. Now fear of an uprising among the men holds him to the deed. He is sure they will take the lives of all of us if he refuses this sacrifice to Artemis."

"And Achilles?" Iphigenia asked between sobs.

"He will do what he can to save you. The betrothal was, of course, a trick to get you here. Achilles has acted most honorably. Now I must seek your father and make one last plea to his reason." She laid her hands tenderly on the heaving shoulders of the frightened, weeping girl, then left the tent and spoke to the guard there. "I will await here the arrival of the commander-in-chief."

The guard saluted her respectfully.

At last Agamemnon came. "I'm glad to find you here, Clytemnestra," he greeted her, at the same time dismissing the guard. "I have made all arrangements for the bridal sacrifice. Everything is in readiness."

"Your words are fair enough, Agamemnon, but I know of a deeper purpose behind them." She lifted her voice. "Come out of the tent, Iphigenia, and greet your father."

Presently the girl came, her face wet with tears, her eyes wide and terrified.

"Why are you weeping, my daughter? What has occasioned such wild grief? And you look at me as if you saw a monster. What has wrought such change in you?"

"Before she answers your questions, my husband, I have one to put to you. Do you still plan to kill this child?"

"What fiend put this horrible notion in your mind?" Agamemnon managed to sound like one aggrieved.

"Answer my question."

For a moment he stared back at her, then flung up his hands, at the same time raising his eyes heavenward as if he might read there the words that could appease his furious wife.

"Your intent is completely known to me, Agamemnon. Now I make one last plea for our daughter's life. What will you say when men ask you why you killed Iphigenia? Your answer will be in order that Menelaus can have Helen back. For no other reason our child must die. If the army is so anxious for this sacrifice, then let them draw lots among their own children. Better than that, let Menelaus sacrifice his own daughter. Why ours? Search your heart and do not kill this child."

She had hardly finished speaking when Iphigenia rushed forward and flung herself in the dust at her father's feet.

"Oh, my father, listen to me," she pleaded, looking piteously up into his face. He tried to raise her from the ground, but she clung to his knees, a determined supplicant. "If I had the power of Orpheus, who could move stones to tears, I could move your heart to mercy. I remember well how loving you have ever been to me. I have looked forward to the day when, old and careworn, you would come into my house to be nursed and loved by me. It is the most I have ever wanted. Why should Helen touch my life? Don't send me to the world of shadows on her account."

"Never doubt, my daughter, that I love you. Compassion moves me, but it cannot change my determination. I am no slave to Menelaus, and his wife means nothing to me. But all Greece now calls for this war. The army is mad for revenge against Troy for the insult its prince has delivered to us. They would kill all within the House of Atreus if I refused them this sacrifice and the wind that will take our ships to Troy. It is Greece demanding this of us."

With these words, the leader moved past the two women and entered his tent. Mother and daughter stood alone except for the guard, who now reappeared.

"I see some men approaching," said Iphigenia.

"It is Achilles," said her mother.

"Then let me quickly go inside our tent. I am ashamed to look upon Achilles. My betrothal forced upon him humiliates me."

"Never mind all that now," Clytemnestra warned her. "This is no time for fine feelings. If we can persuade Achilles . . ."

She broke off as sounds of shouting reached them.

Achilles hurried up. "Do you hear that?" he asked. "That sound is the Greek host shouting for the blood of your daughter."

"Was there no one to speak in her defense?" demanded the queen.

"I tried," said Achilles, "and risked death by stoning. My own men were the first to threaten me."

"Then we are lost," declared Clytemnestra.

"Men will come here by the thousands, led by Odysseus, and drag your daughter to the altar. But I shall fight him for her life as I have promised to do."

"These are brave words," said Clytemnestra.

Despite her mother, Iphigenia in shyness and shame had fled into their tent. Now she emerged from it slowly and advanced to where Achilles and her mother stood. She spoke with quiet determination, her head held proudly, all trace of tears gone.

"Listen to me, Mother. It is right that we should give thanks to this brave man for his wish to help us. But for him to stand and fight would accomplish nothing—rather it would bring ruin on himself. So I have come to a decision. I see it all differently now. And my mind is made up.

"I accept my death. And now that I have made up my mind, I want to die nobly, if I can."

Clytemnestra took a step toward her, and Iphigenia stepped back. "No, Mother, do not try to weaken my resolve. I will die for Greece. Only I can give these ships the wind that will take them to Troy. It is I, and not our warriors, who will have caused her fall. I will save Greece, and my name will be honored for all time. What is my life against the lives of the thousands gathered here? To save one little life there will be woeful bloodshed, and this fine man here, fighting bravely for me, will surely be killed. Nor will you and I escape with our lives. No, no, my Mother. Much better that I should yield up my body in willing sacrifice so that our warriors can proceed to Troy and conquer it."

Achilles, reaching out, seized her hand and held it close. "Ah, what a bride would have been mine had destiny so willed it. Greece can be proud that you belong to her. Would you had belonged to me! You are an honor to your house. Still I long to save you."

Iphigenia smiled at him and shook her head. "You must not die for me. Save yourself now and die for Greece."

Achilles dropped her hand. "I leave you now, but remember, if at any moment at the altar your resolve weakens, turn to me, for I shall be close to you, and I will make my promise good." With these last words, he departed from the two women.

They entered the tent together, and now it was Iphigenia who comforted her weeping mother. "Don't weep for me, dear one," she said. "Think only of the glory I shall bring to Greece and to our name. And don't put on mourning for me."

Clytemnestra clasped her child frantically to her. "I will go with you to the altar. My face shall be the last you gaze upon."

But Iphigenia shook her head. "No, let me go alone with the men my father will send for me. You can give me no comfort, and it would trouble me to have you there, enduring such agony."

The tent flap opened and a hesitant guard saluted and said, "I have come for you, my lady."

Iphigenia took her mother's face between her hands and kissed her gently. Twice more she kissed her. "Those two were for my sisters. Do not put them in mourning for my sake. Let them think of me with joy and pride. Farewell."

She turned quickly, and her slim body brushed past the guard, who held the tent open for her. Immediately guards formed on either side of her. A garland was placed on her shining head. Walking steadily, she went toward the meadow where the altar of Artemis awaited her.

Bravely she mounted the steps to where her father and the high priest stood.

Agamemnon placed his hands upon her shoulders. "You are brave, my daughter."

Below them, across the spreading meadow and all along the shore, the Greek fighting men were gathered in a vast body. Silence settled over it as the priest moved toward the girl, a knife in his hand. Agamemnon released her and the priest took her by the arm. He led her to the darkly stained stone where the blood of countless victims had been spilled. All was hushed, expectant. At the direction of the priest, she gracefully lowered herself to her knees and laid her head upon the stone, exposing her slender neck.

Suddenly the priest raised his arm, there was a flash like lightning as the sun caught the blade before its swift descent. There was no outcry from the victim, only her bright blood spilling across the altar. Artemis had been appeased.

A few hours later a gentle wind began to ruffle the smooth surface of the harbor. It grew in strength and it was from the right quarter. The chiefs began bellowing orders. Warriors hurried aboard their ships while sailors sprang to their stations.

Agamemnon hurried to Clytemnestra's tent to take a last farewell of his queen. He was met by the old slave to whom he had entrusted the second letter.

"Queen Clytemnestra has departed for Mycenae," he informed his master. "She left no message."

Agamemnon stood frowning for an instant, then turned and hurried down to the harbor where his ships awaited him. Women were of no consequence now; there was a war to be fought.

THE FALL OF TROY
AND AFTER

*F*or nine bloody years the Greeks and Trojans fought each other on the great plain before the walls of Troy. Sometimes they engaged in single combat when a hero on one side challenged a hero on the other. Sometimes they fought in full force, and then the slaughter was terrible. Sometimes the gods took part in the fray.

Meanwhile, many fine heroes fell. Achilles met the great Trojan, Hector, in single combat and killed him. Then he was, himself, killed by the cowardly Paris—one of the great ironies of the war.

Over the years Paris had become a figure of contempt in Troy. Hector had upbraided him for not taking an equal part in the fighting, and all the Trojans resented him as the cause of the war. Menelaus once challenged him, and in the ensuing fight between them, would have vanquished Paris had not Aphrodite whisked her favorite to safety in a dense cloud. But Paris, too, was at last wounded by one of Heracles' poisoned arrows and died.

In the tenth year Troy fell. A ruse breached her walls where all the fierce frontal attacks had failed.

It was Odysseus who presented to his brothers-at-arms the idea of a wooden horse. His whole scheme was most ingenious. The Greeks should build a wooden horse, he informed them, large enough to hold a sizable group of warriors. When it was ready, it would be wheeled upon the plain in full sight of the city. But before this, the Greek fleet would depart as if giving up the struggle. It would sail to the far side of the island of Tenedos.

One Greek, a man named Sinon, would be left in hiding somewhere near the wooden horse, to be discovered by the Trojans. He was to inform them that the horse was left as an offering to Athena by the Greeks. He was to tell the Trojans that he was to have been a sacrifice to the goddess, but that in the night he had escaped. If the Trojans believed his story (and it sounded a most plausible one), they would in all probability drag the horse inside the city walls. Then when night had come again, the Greek warriors would descend from the horse and, the Greek ships having sailed back to the plain, would open the city's gates to the Greek host.

It all happened exactly as Odysseus had predicted it would. He and several of the best Greek warriors were concealed inside the great wooden horse, awaiting the dawn. The Greek fleet was gone; their camp deserted. When the city awoke, the Trojans could scarcely believe their eyes. But once sure that the enemy had departed, they flocked out of the gates to inspect the marvelous horse and to overrun the Greek camp. It was then Sinon revealed himself to them and told his tale. He was taken at once to Priam, to whom he repeated it. Priam believed his story and even felt sorry for poor Sinon, who now declared that he no longer wished to be a Greek, but a Trojan.

Then the people started hauling the great wooden horse inside the walls. All day they celebrated what they thought was a clear victory. The Greeks were gone and in their place was this most marvelous structure, an offering to Athena. They wined, they dined, they danced. Night came and they took to their beds, exhausted.

It was then that a door in the belly of the horse opened, a ladder was lowered, and the fighting men began to emerge. In minutes the great gates were flung wide and the Greek host surged through them. Troy's doom had arrived. No man of the Trojan force escaped except Aeneas, who later was to found the city of Rome. All the women were parceled out as slaves, Hecuba, Andromache, and Cassandra among them.

Only Helen was spared. With every courtesy and honor, she was escorted by Menelaus to his ship for the long journey home. They were blown off their course and experienced some trials before Sparta was reached. But Helen came safely home at last.

Odysseus suffered the greatest hardships. The prophecy was fulfilled, and he was ten years drifting among the islands and along the distant shores of many seas before he came in the end to his homeland.

The worst fate of all was reserved for Agamemnon. He, too, endured the wrath of Poseidon and lost all but one of his ships. Notice of Troy's fall had been heralded by fires lighted on the tops of hills, the beacons traveling south until at length they could be sighted from the ramparts of the palace at Mycenae. Clytemnestra, who had never forgiven Agamemnon for the sacrifice of his daughter, was apprised of the victory and made ready to receive her lord. When he arrived at last, she greeted him with such pomp that he protested that such a welcome should be accorded only to gods. But she, declaring that nothing could be too great an honor for so renowned a hero, led him to a perfumed bath and proceeded to administer to him with her own queenly hands. But in the midst of this ritual, suddenly she threw a robe about him in such a way that he was rendered defenseless by it. Then, seizing a dagger, she stabbed him to death.

GLOSSARY

Achilles	a kĭl′ēz	Calchas	kăl′kăs
Acteon	ăc tē′ŏn	Cassandra	kă săn′dra
Aeneas	a nē′ăs	Castor	kas′ter
Agamemnon	ăg a měm′nŏn	Cheiron	kī′ron
Agelaus	ăj e lā′ŏs	Clytemnestra	klī těm něs′tra
Alexander	ăl ěg zăn′der		
Andromache	ăn drŏm′a kē	Demeter	de mē′ter
Aphrodite	ăf ro dī′tē	Diomedes	dī o mē′dez
Apollo	a pŏl′ō	Dioscuri	dī ŏs kŭ′ri
Argives	ar′gīvs	Domophoön	dō mōf′ō ōn
Argonauts	ar′gō nawts	Doris	dor′ĭs
Athena	a thē′na		
Atreus	ā′trē ŭs	Eris	ěr′ĭs
Aulis	o′lĭs	Euboea	ū bē′a
Boeotia	bē ō′sha	Gemini	jěm′ĭ ni

Hades	hā′dēz	Paris	păr′ĭs
Harpie	har′pee	Peleus	pē′lūs
Hector	hĕc′tor	Pelion	pē′lĭ ŏn
Hecuba	hĕk′u ba	Penelope	pē nĕl′ō pē
Hellespont	hĕl′ĕs pŏnt	Perseus	pur′sūs
Heracles	her′a klēz	Polydeuces	pŏl ĭ dū′sēz
Hermes	hŭr′mēz	Poseidon	po sī′don
Hermione	hur mī′o nē	Priam	prī′am
Hesione	hē sī′o nē	Prometheus	prō mē′thūs
Ida	ī′da	Scamander	ska măn′der
Idas	ī′dăs	Scyros	sī′ros
Iphigenia	ĭf ĭ jē nī′a	Sinon	sī′nŏn
Iris	ī′rĭs	Sparta	spar′ta
		Styx	stĭks
Jason	ja′sŭn		
		Telemachus	tē lĕm′a kŭs
Leda	lē′da	Telemon	tĕl′a mon
Lycomedes	lī kō mē′dēz	Tenedos	tĕn′ĕ dŏs
Lynceus	lĭn′sus	Theseus	thē′sūs
		Thetis	thē′tĭs
Menelaus	mĕn ĕ lā′ŭs	Troy	troi
Mycenae	mī sē′nē	Tyndareus	tĭn dā′rē ŭs
Mycaenean	mī sē nē′ăn		
		Zeus	zūs
Nereides	nē rē′ĭ dēz		
Nereus	nē′rūs		
Odysseus	o dĭs′ūs		
Oenone	ē nō′nē		
Olympus	ō lĭm′pŭs		
Orestes	ō rĕs′tēz		

ABOUT THE AUTHOR

DORIS GATES was born and grew up in California, not far from Carmel, where she now makes her home. She was for many years head of the Children's Department of the Fresno County Free Library in Fresno, California. Their new children's room, which was dedicated in 1969, is called the Doris Gates Room in her honor. It was at this library that she became well known as a storyteller, an activity she has continued through the years. The Greek myths—the fabulous tales of gods and heroes, of bravery and honor, of meanness and revenge—have always been among her favorite stories to tell.

After the publication of several of her books, Doris Gates gave up her library career to devote full time to writing books for children. Her many well-known books include *A Morgan for Melinda* and the Newbery Honor Book, *Blue Willow*.